Worley Faver - Artist & Potter
"Spirit-Man"

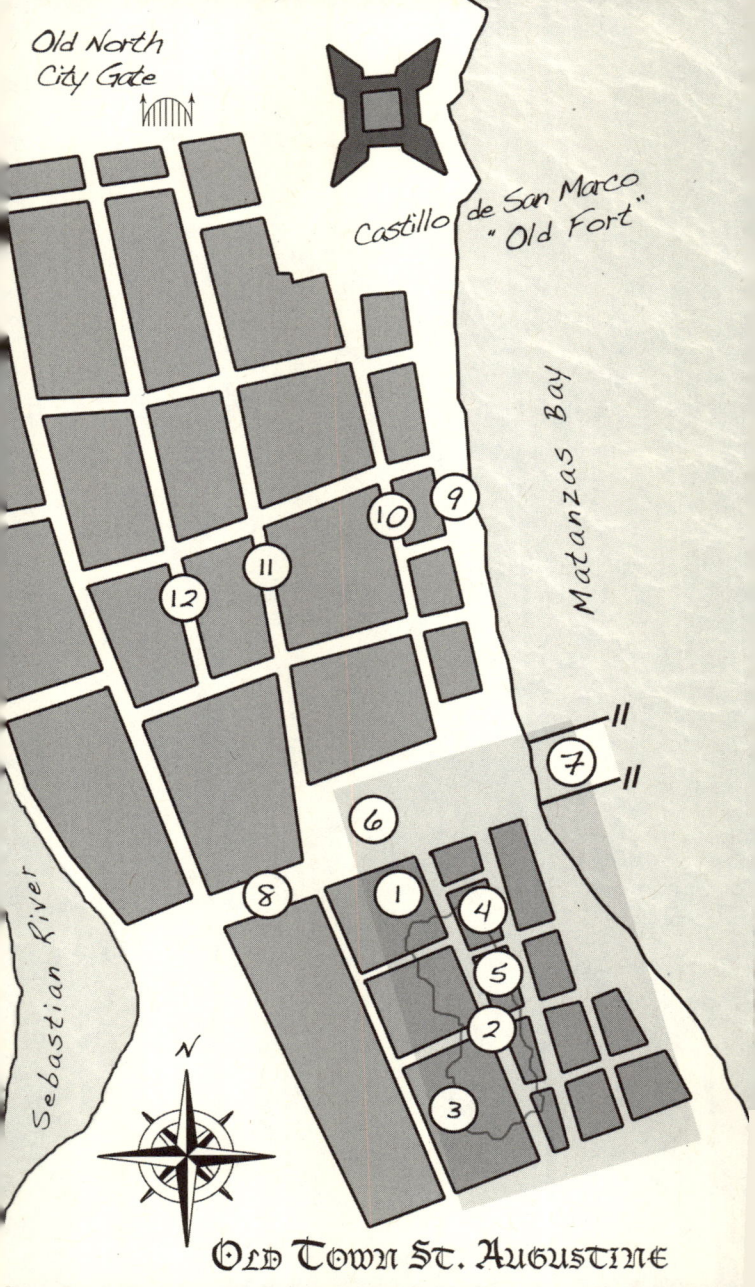

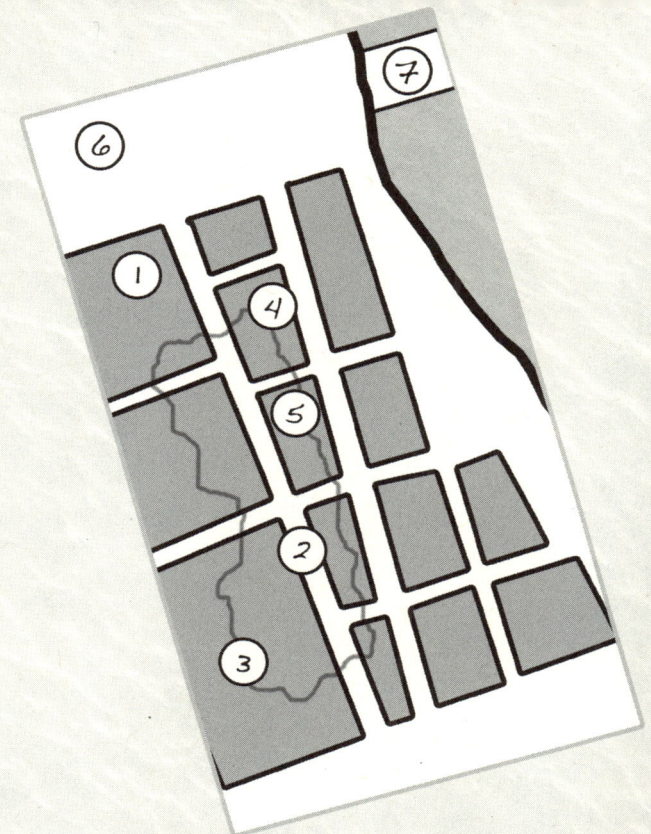

1. Potter's Wax Museum
2. Aviles Street
3. Timucuan Burial Mounds
4. Old Spanish Military Hospital
5. Worley Faver Pottery Studio & Gallery
6. Plaza
7. Bridge of Lions
8. King Street
9. San Marco Avenue
10. Charlotte Street
11. St. George Street
12. Spanish Street

Potter's People

Potter's People
& the
Ancient Spirits of Aviles Street

by
Dennis M. Smith, Jr., M.D.

This book is a work of fiction. Names, characters, places, and incidents are products of the author's imagination or are used fictitiously. Any resemblance to actual events or locales or persons, living or dead, is entirely coincidental.

Copyright © 2012 by Local Legends Press

Published by Local Legends Press

Printed in Canada.

All rights are reserved to the publisher. No part of this publication may be reproduced or transmitted in any form or by any means, electronic or mechanical, including photography, recording, or any other information storage and retrieval system, nor may the pages be applied to any materials, cut, trimmed, or sized to alter the existing trim sizes or matted or framed with the intent to create other products for sale or resale or profit in any manner whatsoever, without prior permission from the publisher.

ISBN: 978-0-9832869-3-6

Dedication

To my niece, Alexandria Ramsier, and my mother-in-law, Lynn Benner, my greatest fans and my only two relatives who actually read what I write!

Acknowledgments

Creative Design
Dennis M. Smith, Jr., M.D.
Rylan Love

Cover Design, Book Layout, Digital Editing
Rylan Love

Editors
Tania M. Bourdon
Dennis M. Smith, Jr., M.D.

Publisher
Local Legends Press
St. Augustine, Florida

Photography
Stephanie McIntyre

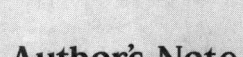

Author's Note

Special thanks to…

Worley Faver, my great friend and fabulous potter, who was my inspiration for finally figuring out how to end the ghostly feud on Aviles Street. As much as I hate to admit it, the description of Worley in this book is really true!

Kimber Lee Ponce and Hope Chessel at Potter's Wax Museum for answering my endless inquiries, providing research for this story, and allowing us to have access to the museum whenever we needed it.

The Aviles Street Merchants Association, whose wonderful galleries, shops, and eateries on this lightly traveled street are St. Augustine's best kept secret.

All the ghosts and spirits of this special piece of earth we call St. Augustine— it's a great town in which to live or visit. I imagine they all agree!

Tips on Reading My Poetry

There are no formal rules on how to read poetry, at least not that I can find. I always prefer practical solutions, so if you would like some guidelines on reading this story and poetry in general, let me offer several suggestions. By the way, if your favorite literature teachers or professors disagree with what I write here, I would recommend that you follow their more professional opinions—mine are purely based on my personal experiences and writing styles.

To me, the underlying beauty of poetry results from the sound of the rhymes and the rhythm. Thus, this book should be read aloud whenever possible. If you prefer an audience when reading aloud but do not have one, then pronounce each word silently to yourself. Most importantly, please read with emotion, intensity, and variable volume. Make believe you're the narrator of a motion picture or an actor on Broadway. Use accents if you can. Mostly, have fun! Poetry is not intended for speed reading, and these tips may help to slow you down and absorb what you are reading. Take your time and enjoy the considerable energy and effort that the author expended to create rhymes and rhythm.

Rhythm, or the pace and meter of a poem, can be defined in classic terms (e.g., iambic pentameter) that are taught in school. In my stories, I use rhythm and pace to add emotion, effect, and emphasis. I do not necessarily keep the "meter" and pace constant throughout the piece; rather, I use it as a tool to enhance the emotion created by that specific passage in the story.

I use punctuation, or a lack of it, as hints and keys to help control the pace or tempo. Let's consider how the following punctuation marks indicate pauses as you read this poetry aloud:

Periods indicate the end of a thought and suggest a full stop (a relatively long pause).

Colons indicate a dramatic, almost full pause and "clue-in" the reader that an

important clarifying piece of information is about to be read.

Dashes separate phrases in a sentence to indicate a prolonged pause before the continuation of an important, clarifying statement or to indicate an abrupt change in thought.

Semicolons indicate medium length pauses between two complete and related concepts.

Commas indicate brief pauses between words, phrases, or compound sentences.

Ellipsis points (…) indicate a long pause and prime the reader that a few very important words follow immediately.

No punctuation means just keep on truckin', even at the end of a line. If there is no comma or other punctuation mark, the author intends for you to read the next line as if it were printed on the same line as the one immediately before it. In fact, several lines may be read with no pauses of any kind, so take a deep breath when there is punctuation that gives you a pause.

In addition to punctuation, I also use other clues for the reader. As with most text that we read, italics, bold, and underline are used to emphasize words or phrases. Indenting a line or series of lines indicates that the indented segment is subordinate and related to the topic immediately above it that is not indented. In addition, a space between passages suggests that a new thought, concept, or topic (think of them as paragraphs) within the chapter is being introduced.

As a last thought, I love writing in rhyme because, in the final analysis, there are no rules. As a result, some may argue that what I write isn't "real" poetry. Yet, my style allows me to write in incomplete sentences (although I try not to…my favorite English teachers, Mrs. Moseley and Mrs. Boise, would not approve), make up words to form a rhyme, use grammatically incorrect punctuation to have an impact on

the rhythm, and change meter whenever I wish.

All of these "no-no's" I can do under the auspices of "poetic license." Ain't it great!

I hope these suggestions help! If you have other thoughts that would assist future readers in gaining the most enjoyment from my writing, please e-mail your ideas to me at swamphattie.com or locallegends.com.

 ## Read This

For all comments that I incorporate into future versions of "Tips on Reading My Poetry," I will acknowledge the contribution in future books and send you a free copy of my most recent story. In advance, thank you for your help!

Poetic License in *Potter's People*

Keep your eyes open for the following examples of poetic license in *Potter's People*:

Hobnoblins is not a real word, but it should be! I have used this term in stories and poems for years, and everyone seems to know what these small, gnarled, deformed, mischievous dwarf-like creatures are. Don't you?

Extra-vital is derived from "extra-" meaning "outside of" or "beyond" and "vital" meaning "of life" or "characteristic of life." Thus, this term translates to "beyond life" or "outside of life." This term evolved as a result of my need to create a short acronym for all sorts of ghostly hauntings and events. See below.

EVP (Extra-Vital Phenomena) refers to any and all paranormal events, including sightings, sounds of unknown origin, auto-locomotion of inanimate objects, increased electromagnetic measurements, etc.

although existing terms could have been used, most of these words are polysyllabic or must be used in groups, facts that wreak havoc with rhyme and rhythm. **EVP** is born!

Telepathicized, like hobnoblins, also defines itself within its context. From "telepathy" or "telepathic," I'm certain you get my message without me speaking a word!

Seeked is the past tense of seek; yes, I know it is really "sought," but sought doesn't rhyme with "tweaked" and "techniques."

Vociferences is another new "word" spawned by the necessity to find a rhyme for "differences" with a meaning that connotes "vociferousness." After literally hours of working and reworking this passage, I gave up and coined the new term.

Joast …well, this explanation is embarrassing but true. I have used this "word" all of my life. I did not discover that it was not a "real word" until I wrote this story and needed a word that rhymed with "boasts" and "coast" that would fit the context. When I typed "joast," "Word" redlined it; I thought it was one of those entries that is not included in its dictionary. Only after checking my American Heritage and several online dictionaries and discussing "joast" with a good friend who is far more literate than I, did I convince myself that, somewhere, sometime, somehow I had internalized this "new word." I had always thought that a "joast" was good-natured bantering back and forth between two individuals or groups. Much introspection leads me to conclude that, as a child, I heard reference to "they were only jousting in fun" from someone with a thick southern accent, and, as much as I'd like to deny it, "joast" embedded in my brain.

Ancient Spirits of Aviles Street

Prologue

St. Augustine's Aviles Street, a secret gem of Florida's First Coast
In an Ancient City known for its haints, spirits, and ghosts,
Is studded with great galleries and cool shops, but it can also proudly boast
That it is the New World's most haunted street
Because it is replete
With more contingents of once-living spirits and occasionally seen ghosts
Than any other location between our country's coasts.

Why are there so many ghosts on this short road?
Just who are these spirits, and why is this their abode?
What in this, or any other, world are Potter's People?
Why do they reside almost under the shadows of the steeple
Of one of this town's oldest houses of prayer?
On Aviles Street, these apparitions seem

to be everywhere.
And what do they have to do with the
 Native American Timucuans
And the original Spanish soldiers who
 long ago came and are now gone?
If you wish to know the answers, please
 read on!

The events contained in the following
 story
Come from the dreams of a man named
 Worley—
Vague dreams that he recalls only
 poorly.
But his recollections stirred my interest
 and imagination,
Causing me to research with great
 determination
The history of Aviles Street. Could it's
 past possibly possess the explanation
For the meaning of the visions that
 caused Worley so much consternation?
Please read on, so you, too, can
 understand the facts and foundations
For what finally led me to conclude that

Aviles Street
 … is, in truth, the most haunted street in our New World nation.

You see, Potter's Wax Museum, the Old Spanish Military Hospital grounds,
The New World's first Catholic cemetery only recently found,
And today's structures on Aviles Street
 … *all* disturb an ancient Timucuan burial mound.
Ghosts in this setting are a foregone conclusion.
They are real; they are not some magician's mystical, mythical illusion.
Sightings are frequent; paranormal phenomena, an everyday occurrence—
They are as common as the near-by bay's ebbing and flowing currents.
Confrontation with these beings are so frequent
That paranormal investigators continue to document
The existence of these spirits and these other worldly events.

So it is not surprising that, a few years back,
This street became the setting of gruesome attacks
Between two opposing factions: an invading army of Potter's ghosts
Versus Spanish soldier spirits and their apparitional Timucuan hosts.

Hitler - Nazi Dictator and Murderer

Chapter 1

In the Beginning – The Madame

This tale took roots in London many years ago;
Innocent enough, the Madame just wanted a better show.
She went to the city morgue where the homeless dead go
To examine the body of a departed, ordinary Joe
Who would serve as a model for a celebrity, whom you all have seen and know.
The Madame always selected her models very carefully;
Otherwise she would never achieve perfection successfully.
Each model must possess the correct height, weight, and size;
Each must own the right color hair, skin, and eyes.
She studied them extensively and then hand-crafted every part—
It was her passion, right from the beginning, right from the start.
She assembled all the pieces. Then, she applied German glass eyes, real

human hair,
Handmade costumes, paint, polish, and make-up. And she did it with flair!
These were the easy tasks, but sculpting the body parts left the Madame in despair:
Carving and shaping blocks of hard wax
Took weeks of intense work and revealed the indelible fact
That the Madame must find a better way
To make more realistic figurines without generating so much delay.
What she discovered changed our Madame:
    She became calculatingly cold
      And inhumanely cruel as she grew old.

In an effort to make her mannequins' bodies stronger, more realistic, more bold,
She studied the art of making plaster casts and molds.
But to make a mold, one must first possess a blank;

In our case, a dead corpse or a body part, which, to be quite frank,
Were all too often, decaying, rotting, and rank.
Thus, the Madame and her workers became regulars in the morgue's den of death.
They got used to the stench—they no longer had to hold their breath.
They got used to the fear—their hearts no longer yearned to palpitate.
They got used to the guts and gore— they no longer needed to regurgitate.
They didn't even leave for supper; they just stayed in the morgue while they drank and ate.
Quickly, they learned whole bodies were useless—too hard to manipulate.
They resorted to hacking off the needed part—to mutilate
The corpses of the poor, destitute deceased.
The morgue attendants and dieners cared not in the least,
Just as long as their palms were

occasionally greased.
Neither the morgue workers nor the Madame's own men
Spoke publically of these activities that occurred quite often, not just now and then.

To make molds, the Madame's workers fashioned wooden frames of proper size and shape,
Binding them together with nails, leather bands, and tape.
They filled them halfway with a special plaster-of-Paris they made
Using only the finest ingredients of the very highest grade.
Letting the plaster set to just the right fluidity,
They'd extract a body part and coat it with some acidity
That, when laid onto the plaster,
Would form one-half of a smooth, clean master
Copy of the limb, head, torso, or digit.
Then, when the plaster hardened to the

density of a metallic widget,
They'd coat the level horizontal surface with pure lard
And pour on more plaster and leave it until it was perfectly hard.
The result of the Madame conducting this artistic activity
Was a mold of the object that generated great gains in productivity:

A fast, efficient means of getting just what she desired—
An exact replica, cast after cast, so lifelike she never tired
Of making her molds and filling them with wax,
And so truly realistic she never revealed the facts
That we tell here for the very first time:
Her desire for perfection led her to murder and crime!

Chapter 2

The Search for Perfection

The Madame knew that perfection required models of properly matched size:
Exact measurements of height, weight, chest, waist, hips, and thighs.
There was no margin of error for the color of the hair and the eyes.
With her living subjects, the Madame went to extremes in trying to explain,
Often over dinner or a glass of champagne,
Why she needed such personal details.
She usually succeeded and prevailed;
But, if the celebrity refused, that was not the end of the trail.
She would pay secret spies to buy, steal, or otherwise obtain
The vital measurements of her icon–no secrets remained!
Doctors' records, tailors' charts, personal closets, and discarded trash
Provided what she needed, as long as she had the cash!

Long deceased subjects offered more

challenges still,
But the Madame had the money and she had the will.
She allowed nothing to stand in her way; she would not be impeded.
Public archives often contained just what she needed.
When they didn't, she would personally beg or plead
With relatives for the data to fill her need.
When all else failed, graves and tombs were ransacked and robbed;
Museums were burglarized…absolutely anything to complete her job.

With these critical details in her hands,
The Madame now had even greater demands.
She became pickier about her models' measurements, weights, and heights.
She placed her orders and would not pay unless *everything* was just right.
The goal she pursued was almost there…almost, but not quite.

Yet, for the first time ever, she sensed that perfection was in sight!

Fate then played her hand,
Leading the Madame to understand
That the fresher the corpse,
The less the mold bends and the resulting part warps.
Thus, she initiated endeavors to get the freshest body parts,
So that she could get the best product right from the start.
Remember: "As realistic as possible" was the Madame's goal
And the warmer the body, the better the mold
And the higher the price for which the mannequin sold.

The hospital orderlies grew greedy and bold
In the quest for more pieces of silver and gold.
They brought the bodies for making the Madame's molds

While they were still warm, before they were cold.
Even cool bodies were worthless; they were just too old.
The orderlies and morgue dieners eventually reached a deal
To help the Madame make her wax sculptures look absolutely real:

In return for more money that the two groups would share,
The orderlies would make certain that the morgue was aware
When an indigent patient was on his deathbed.
They would alert the Madame of the opportunity ahead.
In this way, the Madame would be at hand
When the poor soul departed for his promised land.

The more the Madame met success, the more she refined her techniques.
She pressed hard to achieve the

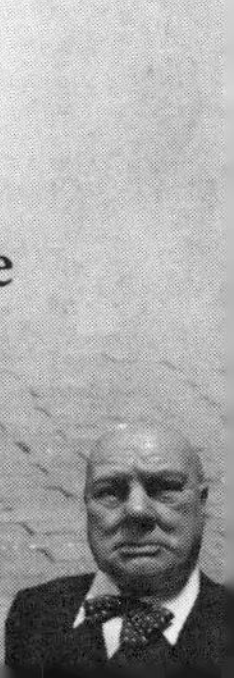

perfection she seeked.
Never quite good enough, she continued to tweak
The plasters and the waxes–any component that was weak.
The molding and casting, she soon conquered outright,
But the final products still failed to provide her delight.

When pondering her dilemma one sleepless summer night,
She cursed her failure, and her temper flared!
She became suddenly, absolutely, acutely aware
Of the sweat on her brow and the sultry evening air.

"I hate this heat; I should go to the morgue to cool my pains."

The stifling heat and humidity were clearly a drain.
As she trudged to the morgue, it began to rain.

SWAMP HATTIE'S LAIR   18

Entering this den of death, she could not refrain
From chiding herself, "Figure this out; use your brain!"
The contrast of the morgue's cold and the summer night's heat
Reminded her that temperature of a body's meat
Was a critical component to complete
The creation of her target feat:
A perfect likeness that was deplete
Of imperfections from the top of its head to the soles of its feet.
The Madame obsessed with accomplishing this feat.

She examined the bodies on the morgues cool slabs—
Feeling a head; the back of a hand; a toe tab—
The temperatures varied greatly depending on where she touched.
Even on a single cadaver, the variation was such
That she wondered if there was a way to

decide
What was the best indicator of a corpse's true temperature? Could it come from *inside*?

For the next thirty days, the Madame conducted an experimental study—
One by necessity grotesque, gross, gory, and bloody.
Every corpse brought to the morgue became part of the analysis,
Which she hoped would end her brain's deep paralysis
In finding the final clue that would lead to perfection.
Her experiment involved developing a method for detection
Of the body's core temperature: the one from *within* the heart.
Reasoning that the surrounding body would act as insulating parts,
The Madame hypothesized that the heart's temperature was the place to start.
To standardize all aspects of her task,

She decided *she personally* would make the molds and wax casts
Of the most difficult element of her job: the death mask.
By standardizing herself as the maker of the art
And by standardizing the face as the body part,
The only variable to affect the quality would be the temperature of the heart!

Her experimental design worked to perfection!
Statistical analysis allowed her detection
Of an undeniable fact:
If she wanted a replica exact,
The heart's temperature must almost be at its height—
Ninety-eight point two degrees Fahrenheit!
Almost the temperature of a living human being!
Cold core body temperatures caused the imperfections she'd been seeing!

The Madame had scientifically proven that the most critical features
To casting the most realistic humans, animals, and creatures
Were obtaining the perfectly sized and shaped body part,
And, more significantly, an almost living temperature in the corpse's heart!
These factors determined the final quality of her wax-casting art!
The solution to her predicament was now simple and clear:
Know your subject's measurements to the smallest tear,
And be close at hand when the model's death was near.

The Madame now offered great economic rewards,
But only for perfect specimens from the hospital wards.
The measurements must fit, and the temperature be just right;
Otherwise, no payments, regardless of

size, weight, or height.
The problem was, this combination of requirements
Could almost never be met by Death's own experiments.
The order of the request was simply too tall…
If restricted to *natural* deaths within the hospital's walls.

Then, one day, an enterprising, young orderly attendant man
Boldly stated, "I have a foolproof plan."
He then related how he often internally debated:
"Would this poor, homeless, helpless soul
Be better off dead than alive in this hospital hellhole?"
Occasionally, he took it upon himself to dispatch the decrepit being,
Which was very easy to do without anyone ever seeing,
Given the city hospital wards were dark and absent of visitors.

AVILES STREET

He grew confident that there would be no inquisitors.
To the head of the morgue, to the Madame, but to no other,
He swore all to secrecy, and, then, he began to uncover
How he could choose patients of just the perfect size, height, and weight
That would allow the Madame to create
The perfection of her passion, of her dreams, of her desires:
She could have the body *before* it expires!

The orderly would select the chosen daughter or son,
According to the Madame's specification, each and everyone.
The "honored guest" would then be secretly drugged and sedated
To such an extent that his death would be simulated.
Given the nature of these street urchins in the city ward beds,
Not even the doctors would check to see

if they were *really* dead!
The plan was concocted and that's just how it transpired:
The Madame could indeed have her subject *before* it expired!

After a short investigational trial,
The Madame knew these efforts were worthwhile!
The casts met perfection in every sense of the word;
The thought of anything better was, well, totally absurd.
Not only that, but she soon discovered,
If one placed her target in the morgue uncovered
And gave it time to begin to recover
From the effects of the drugs that simulated its death,
The victims would initiate long, deep breaths
And regain enough consciousness and mortality
That the Madame could evoke facial originality

By inducing pain or agony, sadness or laughter,
Before sending the model into the hereafter.
Now, not only were the death masks absolutely, technically exact,
But all facial features and expressions could be preserved intact!
By cutting off a living limb or tickling an underarm,
The Madame could capture the face's "charm"
And its last emotional expression, before the victim drowned
In a thick emulsion of plaster that he had no choice but to swallow down.
Imagine! Drowned in plaster
On your way to the hereafter!
Mutilated alive
As the Madame strived
And finally arrived…
At her goal of perfection.
One by one, dozens upon dozens, the Madame executed her crimes.
On those unfortunate living who had

neither pennies, nor nickels, nor dimes.
At their expense, the Madame entered her prime
As a master-caster whose works were sublime,
And as a ruthless, heartless criminal—
one of the worst of all time.

The Madame and her crew continued to refine their art,
Making *life* masks from victims with beating hearts,
Whacking off only what they wanted—
to get that one perfect part—
Whether a head, a face, a hand, or a limb.
They took what they wanted, oblivious to the soul within.

These merciless, living amputations
Created great distress and consternation
For the ghosts of the bodies that were torn asunder.
These spirits wandered and openly

wondered:

"Where are *all* my parts? I must be buried *whole*.
Without all my pieces, I cannot control
My fate or my destiny, and I'll be forced to enroll
In the brotherhood of the lost and searching dead—
To Purgatory, I shall be eternally wed."

Because of this fact, many of these spirits became ghosts
Who stayed with their waxy counterpart hosts—
They had nowhere else to go
With their real bodies having been desecrated so.

If an old figurine cracked and was cast aside,
The spirit had to make a choice; it had to decide,
"Do I stay with my original with whom I died,

Or do I choose a new statue within which to reside?"
Some stayed with the originals; others sided with the new.
There was no way of telling what each would do.
As the Madame's figurines found their way around the earth,
From pole to pole and across its circumferential girth,
The spirits and ghosts spread from London, too,
All thanks to the Madame and her madman crew.

After the Madame passed, her processes continued to last.
A secretive few kept making the Madame's perfect casts
And creating generations of lost souls and ghosts from the past.
As these wax figures were sold, the ghosts' dominions grew vast,
Thanks to the practices that compare and contrast

The sensibilities of most humans who truly care
With those few who simply dare
To do whatever it took
To rewrite the book
Of human decency and respect,
Which they violated in every aspect,
In return for a few shekels of gold—
A story as common as mankind is old.

All of which brings us to one Mr. George L. Potter
Whose wax museum provided the fodder
To ignite a conflict between the ghostly armies and fleets
Of Potter's People and the ancient spirits of Aviles Street.

Chapter 3

Potter's People

The legend of the spirits and pieces of Potter's People
Trace their beginnings to the shadows of a St. Augustine steeple
Where old man Potter, in about 1944,
Sought to acquire, from the Madame's London fabrication store,
Textbook examples of the wax figures he adored.
Mr. Potter was quite eccentric; rather strange, it's been said.
He specifically requested figurines thought to be associated with the living dead!
Mr. Potter subscribed to a unique belief:

Death gives no relief
To those carved in stone or cast in bronze or wax.
These pseudo-deities, God never allows to relax.
The very act of being commemorated in physical form
Creates an irrepressible, negative cosmic energy storm
That morphs into a restless spirit—bad

energy, transformed.
There are exceptions to this norm,
But the majority become ghosts who cannot conform
To the normal order of living and dying—
That was the curse of their deifying
By the likes of the Madame and her mere mortal men
Who did not understand the end, much less where Life begins.

Potter got just what he sought;
Wax figurines from the Madame's own molds he bought.
Dozens and dozens to St. Augustine he brought.
He purchased them tickets on a chartered plane;
Costumed them appropriately to reflect their fame;
Placed them in seats where they had to remain
Secured snugly by bands and straps in order to retain

Their perfection of figure, form, and frame.
As you can imagine, not one complained,
Just like all ordinary Joes and Janes.

Although Mr. Potter was not exactly sane,
About his new wax figurines possessing ghostly remains…
Well, about this little known fact, he was right as rain!
What escaped Mr. Potter in his pursuit of these spirits and their games
Was that these spirit-beings had attached to wax bodies bearing others' names;
Had adopted the persona of the figurine's fame—
Their egos and attitudes were one and the same;
Had assumed an arrogance that could not be tamed—
They were now the privileged, the entitled: everything was *their* game!

They had no guilt; they had no shame.
All because they were associated with a waxen celebrity's name!

Most were obnoxious; they had nothing to gain
By mingling with the Ancient City's infamous bane
Of ordinary ghouls, goblins, and hobnoblins of dark fame.
Potter's Peoples' spirits wanted to be left alone
With their wax figurines—their castles, their sanctuaries, their homes.

Yet, simple squabbles among these beings still occasionally occurred
And disturbed the strict order of the museum that Mr. Potter preferred.
Rare evidence of a confrontation—a broken digit or tousled hair—
Mr. Potter or his assistants easily repaired.
The occasional grunt, growl, or groan
Alerted Mr. Potter and his staff that they

were not alone.
Such events generated rumors and innuendos
About the ghosts that resided within his museum's windows.
The lack of factual sightings dismayed Mr. Potter,
Who secretly was a planner and a plotter
Who desired to be "haunted" so he could use it as fodder
To fuel attendance at his museum.
He absolutely knew people would pay to see them—
The statutes and the *souls* he had spirited to this "City of Old;"
Unfortunately, he never discovered the key, and his museum eventually sold.

Mr. Potter went to his grave heavily grieving
For proof of what he had always been believing
That his Potter's People were the ghosts that lived within the wax.
His heart and head held that truth, but

only historical facts
Would eventually resolve all doubt and, finally, redact
The opinion that Mr. Potter was loony and truly insane.
The events since his death irrefutably explain
And undeniably support that the museum with Mr. Potter's name
Is today and has been, since that very first flight,
A gathering place for spirits, ghosts, and beings of the night!

Teddy Roosevelt - 26th President of US

Chapter 4

The Museum Moves

The spirits of Potter's People settled into a simple routine
Of existence attached to their famous figurines,
Content to be occasionally heard but rarely seen.
They kept to their own, never mingling with the other ghosts
That make St. Augustine famous from coast to coast.
The darkness of the wax museum suited them well,
As it reminded them of London when the fog and mist fell.
They found comfort here, more so than any B&B or old hotel.

What changed, you might ask, that altered this equation
And brought stress, strain, and duress to Old Town's spiritual nation?
As often happens in this interesting world of ours,
Unexpected, chance events—*Fate* is a mysterious power—

Intervene and propel us on a new course,
Driven by the winds of change and an uncontrollable force
To a destination never charted or planned.
Such is the plight of mere mortal man.
Our beings of the night, suspended in their Purgatory,
Share similar fates in their never-ending story.
In this case, Mr. Potter decided to divest.
This decision directly led to the ensuing conflicts and unrest:
The new owners of the museum
Created a New World Roman coliseum
By moving the wax figures and their displays
To a new location, not so very far away,
But into a building located on sacred Native American ground—
An ancient, hallowed Timucuan burial mound
Where Native American spirits could always be found.

Outside apparitions' trespassing here
  brought consequences so profound
That few dared violate this small
  sanctuary within Old Town.
Like most Native Americans, the
  Timucuans, being a kind and peace-
  loving tribe,
Had suffered more transgressions than
  can be described.
Thus, tolerance for strangers rarely
  existed;
Their view of outsiders as foreign
  invaders had persisted
Since the arrival of Spain's galleons,
  armies, and priests
Had inextricably altered their lives and
  destroyed their peace.

*The arrival of Potter's People in the
  building at Aviles and King Street
Brought the second invasion of an
  apparitional army destined to compete
For the Timucuan's cherished burial
  ground retreat.
The first challenge was not nearly so*

subtle or discrete,
But, as with all confrontations, there were few choices: fight, negotiate, or retreat.

Samuel Clemens - Author
"Mark Twain"

Chapter 5

The Spanish Military Hospital

Located at 3 Aviles Street in the current Ancient City,
A renovated, cobblestoned lane that is now quite pretty,
Is the "Old" Spanish Military Hospital, about one block from St. Augustine's Bay
A replica of the Royal Hospital of Our Lady of Guadalupe.
The Spanish erected the original in 1784
Without regard for the burial ground of the Timucuans who came before.
They desecrated and violated this holy earth without regard
For the Native American people who had toiled so hard
To eke out a life and meaningful existence
In a harsh land that only grudgingly provided subsistence.
The construction process disturbed ancient graves,
Releasing restless spirits of chiefs, warriors, and knaves.
These ghosts resented these Spanish

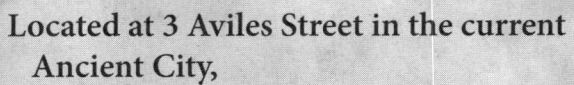

crusaders
Whom they viewed purely as foreign invaders—
Unwelcomed guests who behaved like tomb raiders.
Most of the Timucuan spirits cared not for revenge.
They just desired peace. But a few on the radical fringe
Declared to retaliate via a haunting binge
Designed to distress the patients, staff, and occupants
Of this ill-placed, man-made medical monument.

These hauntings included sensory events—sightings and sounds—
And auto-locomotion of objects on the hospital's grounds.
Violence was taboo;
Physical harm Timucuans would only reluctantly do,
As they were a kind, peace-loving people who,

Even in death, preferred tolerance
To confrontation and belligerence.
These extra-vital intrusions were intense at first,
But gradually became less as the Timucuans realized the worst:
Their sacred, hallowed burial ground would never be the same;
These diggers would never return to from where they came.

To make matters even worse,
The Spanish did something truly perverse:
Ignoring the soil's clues of human bones and pottery shards,
They built their own Catholic cemetery yard
Right on top of a Timucuan mound!
Enough was enough! These spirits decided to defend their ground.
They could take no more insults from these European fools
Who destroyed their holy graves with ordinary digging tools.

With the very first burial of a Spanish
 infantry man,
The Timucuan spiritual nation had
 taken more than it could stand.
Its Council of Elders decided to act
 before things got out of hand:

> The Timucuans disinterred the corpse
> from a fresh Spanish grave,
> Disemboweled the body, and recited
> expressive chants, rants, and raves
> That caused the ghost of the poor soul
> to be released from the ground
> And to be cursed with the fate of
> having to wander around
> For all eternity, with no rest ever to be
> found.

These events were repeated with every
 single Spanish soldier's demise.
The authorities first blamed "wild
 animals" for the gory surprise;
Then, "grave robbers" who must be
 digging for some buried prize.
To find the facts, they stationed a pair of
 priests as after-dark spies.

The Timucuans decided these padres
should see a real show,
So they could return and tell everyone
where they should never, ever go.
The priests stood stunned both by what
they saw and what they did *NOT* see—
A disinterment and disembowelment by
an *invisible* posse!
It was a site more suitable for a terrorist,
Hun, or Nazi.
The priests shuddered, shook, and
screamed like banshees,
As they rapidly departed in order to flee
To their perceived sanctuary
Of the church's hallowed hall
Where they confessed to the Monsignor
all they could recall
Of the night's supernatural events.
Between shivers and tears, which they
could not prevent,
They described in great detail only what
Hell could have sent.
As the priests mumbled and their
coherence came and went,
The parish's leader demanded, "Have

you been in the sacrament?"
Finally, stumbling and stammering to finish their tale,
The pair broke down and began to wail.
Disgusted by what he had seen in these two disciples of the church,
The Monsignor was determined to do his own clandestine research.
He arrived at the cemetery at the stroke of midnight;
Six Timucuan spirits appeared in the moonlight.

> "We tire of your intrusions into our burial site.
> This is our resting place; you have absolutely no right
> To disturb our peace. It is black and white.
> Please, cease and desist. Now, leave, forthright!"

The Timucuan apparitions vanished without waiting for a reply,
The Monsignor fell to his knees and raised his head to the sky:

"Dear God, what just occurred?
I know my priests' words were stuttered and slurred,
But their story's details were sharp, not blurred.
Now, my brains are spinning, and my emotions, spurred.
While I find this thought truly absurd,
Could we possibly be wrong and this heathen herd ...*right*?"

The Monsignor knew the answer to his prayer:
The clues had been obvious; they had been everywhere.
He immediately ordered the very next day,
Without ever revealing *why* he had to say,
That no more bodies be buried in the ground
In this part of St. Augustine's old town.
But the damage had been irreparably done;
Literally hundreds of soldier ghosts now

had free run
Of the home turf of the deceased
　Timucuans—
Their peace and solitude was…
　forever… gone.

Mary I - Queen of England
"Bloody Mary"

Antiques & Uniques Collectibles

Chapter 6

Soldier Ghosts versus Timucuan Hosts

Apparition versus apparition; ghost against ghost—
The soldiers' spirits battled their unwilling hosts.
The moans and groans thundered on the coast.
Human observers knew not what to say
As static sparks and flashes lit up the bay.
Neither side was willing to budge an inch.
The ghosts grew grumpier than the Christmas Grinch.
After weeks and weeks of fruitless frights and endless fights,
The Timucuan chief recognized this as a hopeless plight:

The soldier spirits fought fiercely to protect their position,
As if the *soldiers* possessed the ammunition—
Not the Native American Timucuan apparitions—
Supplied by defending the inherent condition

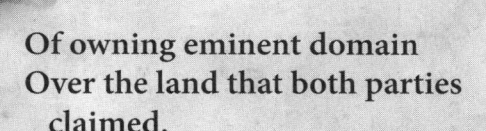

Of owning eminent domain
Over the land that both parties
  claimed.

With that reality fixed in his mind,
The chief sought a truce with the spirits
  of the other kind.
The leader of the soldier spirits was like
  all his brothers—
A mere mercenary foot fighter: no rank,
  no authority, born to an unknown
  mother.
He was, though, savvy enough to see
That he should take this offered
  opportunity
To explore the potential feasibility
Of ending this conflict and achieving
  tranquility.

When the Timucuan chief extended the
  branch,
The Spanish foot soldier leader took the
  chance,
Put down his guard, and relaxed his
  stance:

"You are a spirit of honor; I sense that is true."

The chief responded:

"I ascertain the same of you.
In the absence of mortality,
Let's use this small degree of commonality
To examine what else we share. If we fail, both the majority and minority,
Face endless violence and strife and uncertainty.
I would rather form a union of fraternity
Then continue with this confrontation for eternity."

"Now, let me begin, as this is our native land.
Please bear with me; I want you to understand.
My people came here, after the beginning of Man,
To settle in this hostile, swampy coastal space.

No other tribe wanted this forsaken place.
We loved its solitude, its isolation, its glorious simplicity.
It was unique; there was no duplicity.
We took from the land
No more than it could stand.
With it, our people were one.
We cherished it, as we would a son.
It was *ours*…until *your* kind won
With their weapons, horses, and guns.
With our slaughter—
Every man, woman, son, and daughter—
Was buried within these sacred soils
Where we died, but once we toiled.
This dirt is *all* we ever desired.
It is the only possession of which we never tired.
I hope you see why your presence disturbs us greatly:
We have been here from the beginning; we are no "Johnny-come-lately."

"My Timucuan chief
I can identify. I share your belief
That this is a special land.
I, too, know this first hand.
You see, all these ghosts and me—
Well, we are, at last, free.
We were, in life, simply mercenary.
We had no choice, except the military.
We came from nothing. A peso or two from royalty
Was all it took to buy our service and loyalty.
We lived, fought, and died here as we had no choice:
No discussion, no consideration, no voice.
They buried us on your mound
Because it was the closest piece of ground—
The cheapest dirt that could be found.
Note that officers and clergy with holy gowns
Have all been interred on the good side of town.
The powers that "were" considered these

Chapter 7

Class Warfare

The cultures clashed from the first
  inning.
This conflict had nothing to do with
  righteousness or sinning,
But everything to do with who was there
  in the *beginning*.
It soon became clear that all that
  mattered was losing or winning.
Many of Potter's People had acquired
  something none had while living:
Their figurine's lifelong license for
  taking rather than *giving*.

As you now know, an interesting
  phenomenon had occurred among
  Potter's People's ghosts:
Through the years, they assumed the
  characteristics of their once-living
  wax-figure hosts.
The longer Potter's People's spirits were
  attached to their famous personality
  shrines,
The less these destitute beggars, who
  once survived on crimes,
Could remember their origins. They

forgot their roots!
They became privileged, aristocratic spirits, most of whom didn't give two hoots
For any other soul, living or dead—
Their new positions in "life" had gone to their heads!

Contrast that with the forgotten soldiers and their paupers' graves;
Their violent, agonizing deaths, even if they were brave;
Their poverty, never even a single silver coin saved;
And their coarse, banal, military subsistence.
No one cared even of their mere existence.

Remember, too, the ancient Timucuan burial mound,
Disturbed, desecrated, and flattened to the ground
By Spanish conquerors intent on building a town

And a military hospital on top of earth
　where skeletons were found.
The Native American souls of these
　sacred mounds
Clearly possessed eminent domain.
These resident souls only wished to
　maintain
The sole possession they could ever, as
　their own, claim:
This desecrated ground that contained
　their decayed remains.
Their dirt and coquina-based sand, they
　vowed to retain.

"This land is ours; we were here first!
How dare some Johnny-come-latelies
　with a horse-drawn hearses
And no clue of Catholicism or
　Timucuan spiritual verses
Believe they are entitled because of their
　fame, wallets, or purses!"

As more and more of Potter's People
　arrived at the new site,
The native spirits soon learned that the

Potter's People who understood their plight
Represented a distinct minority. The majority had lost sight
Of the fact that their feigned fame and fortune gave them no special rights.

Joseph Stalin - Dictator of Soviet Union

Chapter 8

The Negotiation

The Timucuan and Spanish soldiers joined forces.
They vowed to stand united and never change courses.
They would resist and persist
Until these invaders agreed to cease and desist.
Their veiled threats were not easy to miss,
And, when pushed to the limit, these ancient warriors' could really get pissed.

Cooler heads among Potter's People initially prevailed;
For the moment, confrontation was curtailed.
The fragile peace waxed and waned and entailed
Numerous discussions between both sides,
Instigated and designed by Potter's People to provide
A strategic advantage to their own side.
Potter's People viewed themselves as far

superior
To the pauper peasants who they believed to be intellectually inferior.

Each group selected three representatives.
Two Spanish soldiers and one Timucuan native
Would represent the plaintiffs.
With Potter's People the emotions ran more ablative;
As a result, the militant faction won out.
Selecting Napoleon, Caesar, and Stalin, there could be no doubt
What the goal of Potter's People was all about.
With the likes of moderates Carver, Churchill, and Crockett left out
And the likes of Capone and Hitler wielding much clout,
Potter's People anticipated a very quick route
Of those "squatter" ghosts they despised more than the Allies did Krauts.

Stalin spoke, representing his side of the fence:

"We understand why you may feel we committed an offense.
But, when you analyze it objectively, does that make any sense?
We came here not of our own volition.
We came only because of our undead condition.
We are wedded to our waxen ways
From now and until eternity's final days.
We had no choice but to poach
On your grounds and to encroach
On your territory, as our owner approached
Opening a new museum right next door
To your reconstructed military hospital store.
Surely, you can see that we mean no harm,
Only a peaceful co-existence—no need for alarm.
We love your ancient city and all of its

charm.
We are like you—destined to wander
the earth—
Neither living nor dying nor giving
new birth.
We ask for your tolerance of our
presence.
That is our proposal, in its essence."

The Timucuan chief spoke next.
He presented his case straight from his
text:

"You have trespassed upon sacred
burial grounds.
You know better; you heard our
warning sounds.
We have been here for centuries,
protecting our tombs
From generations of raiders who dig
through our rooms,
Seeking anything and everything from
gold to pottery shards.
They steal what's not theirs as they
excavate our yards.
These people, whether archaeologist

or thief,
Care not that desecration of our soil causes us great grief.
'There's something there for the taking'—that's their only belief.
After our conflict with the Spanish soldier ghosts,
We found peace with their spirits who inhabit our coast.
They realized that we, their Native American hosts,
Lived and died on this land—we loved it most—
Long before they built their now defunct military post.
We learned something, too; these ghosts were like our brothers—
Simple, respectful, hardworking, from commoner fathers and mothers.
No blue bloods or governors or generals died on our mounds.
Only wounded foot soldiers suffered here and were interred in our ground.
They took orders from others; that's

what we found.
It wasn't their idea to build this Spanish town.
In contrast, you Potter's People bring much pomp and circumstance.
With the likes of you, we have nary a chance
To resume our quiet existence unless you change your untenable stance
That you have just as much right to be here as those who came before.
With that attitude, your threat we cannot ignore.
You are apparitions seeking a different level of existence.
We desire only to be left alone in simple subsistence.
Because of who you are now, you can't understand our resistance.
You Potter's People believe you possess great fame and minds,
But you now represent the best and worst of all mankind:

You are the greatest heroes of all time.
You are the greatest villains to

perpetuate crime.
You are the greatest writers of prose
   and rhyme.
You believe you are the alphas…
We know we are the omegas.

We Timucuans were one with the land.
We never took more from our Earth
   than it could stand.
The land and Earth were all we had.
The state of our soldier friends was
   more than sad.
They owned *nothing*, not even their
   clothes, I might add.
When we Timucuans learned of their
   pathetic plight,
We pitied these souls whom we used to
   fight;
We allowed their spirits to reside on
   our site.
So you see,
The soldiers and we
Cherish this small piece of land
Where your wax figurines now stand.
It is ours,

Since man's earliest hours.
Respectfully, we request
That you end your quest.
You are unwelcomed guests."

"Our good spirit friends,
We have no intention to offend.
We want nothing but to attend
To our figurines here in Potter's halls.
We care for nothing outside these four walls.
Surely, that's not too much to ask.
We come in good faith. Please sip from our flask.
Here! Share our cup; drink it.
And take this bag of beads and trinkets;
You'll like them more than gold ingots."

"You can keep your firewater and your worthless beads!
Your gestures are meaningless, except for the contempt they breed!
Invasive plants flourish through roots,

stems, and seeds;
Invading armies, through diversion, deceit, and deeds.
You forget: we have been observing for hundreds of years.
We know your breed—that is our fear!
In the few short weeks you have resided here,
Rumors circulate both far and near
That Potter's Museum is haunted,
All because of the spiritual presence you and yours have flaunted.
People of your heritage know not how to avoid notoriety and publicity.
Just as our genes crave privacy and simplicity,
Potter's People's psyches yearn for the electricity
Generated by false fame and infamy.
Although your wealth and talents are pure alchemy,
You Potter's People cannot leave well enough alone.
You will bring much trouble to our home.

For this reason, we must insist that you go away.
Vacate these waxen temples where you now stay.
Return to your tombs on the far side of the sea.
Take leave of our land; do it *now*! You *must* agree!"

"My Timucuan chief, your eloquence is persuading,
But we have absolutely no intention of invading
Your side of the street or disturbing your peace.
Besides, Potter's owner possesses a long term lease."

"General, you miss my point completely.
Allow me to try one more time, less discretely.
This *is* our side of the street.
The recreated hospital, the museum, the road—all our ancient beat.

You trespass at this very moment.
Your answers, regardless of how cogent,
Cannot, and will not, change that fact or our minds.
You must depart and try to find
Sanctuary in another place or in another time."

"Chief, my patience wanes and my temper waxes,
As your intolerance and reticence severely taxes
My willingness to be reasonable and compromise.
As spirits of Potter's People, you must certainly realize
That we possess all the tools needed to seize this prize.
While violence some of us may actually despise,
My fellow spirits have already voted and authorized
The use of all resources needed to cause your demise.

To try to resist us would clearly not be wise.
We possess the intellect, the leadership, and the reputations.
You cannot possibly compete; there can be no more procrastination.
We seek a peaceful co-existence,
But I now grow tired of your persistence
That we desert these figures made from our own body parts.
To make their casts they tore off our limbs and cut out our hearts.
We were still alive when they initiated their black art.
We still had breath and pulses beating at the start.
We felt their cold hands; we felt the deep pain.
We suffered for *their* ill-gotten gains.
That's why we have chosen to remain
With the likenesses created by that Madame's demented brain."

"Your tale is touching; your origin belies what you now be.
Your past cannot excuse your present behavior, your arrogance, your treachery.
But it causes me to pause, to reconsider our decree.
I must reconvene our Elder Council because I must see,
If this newly discovered knowledge changes the equation
And warrants our reconsideration of your current situation.
In the interim, please keep your group under control.
I will have my side on patrol
To make certain that no one disturbs even one soul.
We want no more attention brought to our location;
We need no intrusions on our spiritual world nation.
I shall return at midnight after our deliberation."

Chapter 9

The Council of Elders

As one might imagine, the council's meeting caused quite a stir.
The interrogation of the chief came fast; it was truly a blur.
Other Timucuan spirits and soldiers' ghosts also attended,
But not one of them or any council member pretended
To have all the answers or to profess what would be best.
They listened intently to their leader's request
To consider the new information he would present.
They trusted him to be objective and to portray no hint
Of what result would make him most content.
His orations stirred much emotion and sentiment
Both pro and con. Here is a summary of how things went:

The first major issue involved their attitude.
How could any being who died

destitute in such solitude
Show so much arrogance and lack of gratitude,
Simply because one of his body parts helped to recreate
Someone considered special or, in some other way, great?
How could merely being associated with the effigy of a villain
Or the statue of a star such as Matt Dillon,
Or the likeness of some famous good or bad elf,
Or, for that matter, even the living celebrity person himself,
Bestow upon a being the right to claim love or hate?
To claim beauty or fame? To claim *any* of his traits?
This attitude based on what one possessed or whom they know
Bothered the council significantly, and that fact showed.
The other major problem—the preeminent one—revolved around

trust.
How could these beings, who had been returned to dust,
Be counted on to keep their promises and their word?
To think so, most attendees felt was absurd.
After all, these spirits had already encroached
Upon Timucuan territory without ever having broached
Their intentions with those already residing there.
And the Timucuan leaders had made them perfectly aware
That Potter's People's intrusion onto the ancient burial mound
Would be a violation of the Timucuan sacred ground.
Obviously, these Potter's People ignored the owners' rights
And proceeded to occupy this revered site.
Furthermore, these spirits even threatened to use all their might,

In a battle of ghosts in a spiritual fight,
To maintain control of something to which they had no right.
The Timucuans and soldiers lacked meaningful trust,
A feeling virtually all concluded was certainly just.

The debate boiled down to a few considerations
For the spirit soldiers and the Timucuan nation:

Should Potter's People's hardships before they deceased,
Require that special privileges to them be bequeathed?
Should the fact that they suffered poverty and social exclusion
Be considered in the Timucuan's ultimate conclusion?
Should the fact that they lived with discrimination and died with pain
Be an excuse for their unacceptable behavior and allow them to retain
Something that belonged to others?

And more questions remained:
Did they have the right to take what others owned?
Did they have the right to eat the food others had grown?
Or should they be responsible for the seeds they'd sown?
They had chosen to make the flight on which they'd flown.
They had chosen to take over someone else's home.
These facts were difficult for the elders to condone.
After all, *every* Timucuan and Spanish soldier had faced great strife
…while each was living his *own* life.

Chapter 10

Impasse

With neither side willing to budge an inch,
Predicting the inevitable became a cinch.
Negotiations for compromise disintegrated,
As each side became more adamant and agitated.
The more one side challenged the other, the more the other denigrated
The opposite side, until both parties truly hated
Each other, whom they openly berated.
Despite being kindred spirits condemned to Purgatory,
They each had no tolerance for the other side's story.

Were more suited for thinking great thoughts of nuclear fission,
Or leading huge masses of commoners on epic missions,
Or preaching to others about their future visions,
Or making critical earth-shaking, world-changing decisions.
Potter's People's plans needed no revisions—
They just failed to make any provisions
For the fact that they clearly lacked…
Foot soldiers to conduct the final phase of their attack.

The squatter spirits of the hospital grounds
Stood in stark contrast to their foes from London town.
Both the Timucuan spirits and the military ghosts
Built their lives around physical battle and, foremost,
Understood that survival didn't always equate

To the size of one's army or the plans
  one makes.
Their tough lives had honed their
  survival instincts.
To put it bluntly and to make it succinct,
They followed no rules; no prisoners
  they'd take.
Guerilla warfare and sabotage—they
  would not hesitate
To do anything to ensure they'd retake
Their ground. Their graves, they would
  never remake.
Masters of none, they were, in fact,
  masters of Fate.
Something Potter's People never
  realized until it was too late.

Chapter 12

Potter's People Strike!

The great generals of Potter's People had a blood thirst.
They dove in head long, striking hard, striking often, striking first.
They executed plans they carefully rehearsed
Using technology on which they were especially well versed
And which the Timucuans always hated and eternally cursed.
Potter's People dealt such crushing blows
To their primitive, spiritual foes
That the Timucuans and soldiers dissolved and dispersed.
What's more and, probably, worse,
It left these defenders completely submersed
In fears and doubts
After their merciless route:
Could they ever hope to return to the hallowed grounds
Of their ancient, sacred burial mounds?

Chapter 13

Guerilla Warfare!

Following the Timucuans' and Spanish soldiers' stunning defeat,
Potter's People celebrated incessantly their military feat,
But Potter's People overlooked something profound:
Their enemy was defending sacred, hallowed ground!

Having heard enough of Potter's People's pontifications
And viewing defeat as an unacceptable situation,
A Timucuan warrior initiated the first covert confrontation
By breaking the fingers from Napoleon's left hand.
He threw them down on the floor, a gauntlet for all to understand
That his side still feared no one, even this giant little man.
The very next evening, a stealthy spirit shredded Caesar's cape
And covered Stalin's mouth with silver duct tape.

These lightning strikes against Potter's militant faction
Continued on a regular basis, much to the dissatisfaction
Of all of Potter's People, who immediately called for the liquefaction
Of the cowardly Timucuan and soldier ghosts
Who now tormented them incessantly in their one-time haven on Florida's First Coast.

As the spirits of Potter's People observed these dastardly acts,
They turned up the rhetoric and vowed to renew their attacks.
But where was the enemy—its army, its cavalry horses,
Its artillery, its navy, its air forces?
Before Potter's People could figure out *how* to react,
Another fearless Native American proceeded to extract
The gleaming white teeth from Samuel Clemens' warm smile

And dash them against the museum's hard floor tiles.
They severed Moses' arm, and it's never been found.
They dislocated Michelangelo's neck and turned his head around.
Now even the moderates were at risk
Because of the failed militant policy that continued to persist.

The Timucuan and soldier spirits had initiated guerilla warfare.
The patricians among Potter's People became acutely aware
That their presence at Potter's threatened the welfare
Of their shrines—their wax-cast figurines.
Their refuges, once private, safe, and perfectly pristine,
Were now vulnerable targets, easily seen
By renegade spirits who fervently relied
On the fact that this site of their deaths and their family ties
Was their *only* prize

For their having lived and ultimately died.
They had nothing to lose—fate was on their side.
As one might surmise,
This came as a great surprise
To most of Potter's People who continued the reprise:

"We have every right to be here.
We want to make that fact perfectly clear.
Besides, you have everything to fear.
If we so choose, we could summon our peers
From all locations far and near.
You would be vulnerable from the flank and the rear.
You have neither the mentality nor the gear
To compete with our superior forces.
You lack the leadership and the resources."

Potter's People had underestimated their foe:

These plebian spirits had seen it all
 come and seen it all go.
The conquering armies and fleets,
Each had won and, then, met defeat.
The wealthy governors had led and,
 then, died in retreat.
The squatter soldiers' spirits knew time
 was on their side;
They, too, had had nothing to lose since
 they died.
They would protect their only tangible
 possession—
The land where they had taken their last
 confession.
Mercenaries at heart, it was their only
 profession.
In spite of the opposition's rhetoric, they
 kept up the heat
In an attempt to force Potter's People
 into retreat.

As the hostilities once again intensified,
The EVPs were significantly magnified.
The museum's paid staff grew
 progressively horrified

At the grotesque inhuman groans,
The mournful morbid moans,
And the monotonous humdrum undertones
That served as incessant reminders that they were not alone
On these ancient burial grounds that the squatter spirits called home.

Potter's People assumed a defensive stance.
They dared not take the chance
Of crossing old Aviles Street
To confront or otherwise meet
The squatters they wished to displace and unseat.
The risks were simply too great
For these formal ghosts to participate
In a battle of terrorist hit and run tactics.
Such an effort's results would have been tragic,
For they lacked guerilla experience, and they possessed no magic.
Potter's People recognized this reality

And resigned themselves to this finality.

The beings of the military hospital and the native burial grounds
Continued their attacks marked by their terrible sounds.
One of Mussolini's arms went missing,
Amidst the whining, chanting, and hissing
Of an ancient Timucuan medicine man
Who conjured magic and evil spells to command
The extraction and removal of his limb.
Then, reciting an ancient Netherworld hymn,
He orchestrated the removal of both of Hirohito's external ears,
An act that accelerated all of Potter's People's fears:
Had they underestimated their enemy's strengths?
Sensing this weakness, these Timucuan apparitions went to long lengths
To press their advantage and give no relief

To the invading gentility who continued the belief
That these spirits derived from mere common man
Could never prevail. Potter's People simply did not understand.

The sneak attacks continued; they took their toll,
Especially on military leaders who once controlled
Immense marauding armies who invaded and patrolled
Once peaceful lands they wished to own.
Stalin, Caesar, and Grant paid for the evil seeds they'd sown:
Missing eyes, crushed legs, broken digits, melted hands—
All attested to the effectiveness of the guerilla band.
They even stripped the beads from Mary I's gown,
Crushed a few, and strew the rest around.
This physical abuse of their wax-cast

shrines
Caused mental fatigue and, just as designed,
These terrorist attacks that disfigured and maimed
Resulted in the spirits believing they felt real pain.

Leonardo Da Vinci - Artist, Inventor, Scientist

Chapter 14

The Truce

After inflicting this damage on these warlords and their figurines,
The squatter snipers extended their attacks to those neutral and liberal and in between.
This natural evolution brought great pressure to bear
On Potter's People's leaders as the moderates declared
That victory would never be won with military might
And that there could be no winners in this guerilla fight.
The moderates demanded a truce and a negotiation
That would result in discussions about terms of remediation,
And, ultimately, in the creation
Of a space within the museum of a neutral nation,
Where Potter's People could reside without facing ablation.
The moderates forced the hawkish ghosts to resign,
And, then, they wasted no time—

The vote was affirmative: their participation would enable
A lasting peace that would be stable.

Securing the direction that he desired,
The Timucuan chief then asked to retire
For a few moments of meditation
Before revealing to his spiritual nation
The identity of his recommendation
Of the Being to lead this mediation.

> "I shall return without too much delay.
> I must make certain of what I'm about to say.
> I must contact a spirit who is not among us today."

The Timucuan chief vanished into another dimension
Where time and space cease to exist and simply become an extension
Of the soul, living or dead
Where few are ever invited to tread.
Those that come are rare indeed.
They are invited back when they have need

For solutions and guidance for special deeds.
Entering this place
Of heavenly space,
The chief merged with the cosmic dust
And revealed his inner most thoughts and ultimate trust
In the guidance he had not yet received.
He possessed faith: he *believed*.

Returning to his council after only a matter of seconds,
The Timucuan chief reached out and quietly beckoned:

"Join me, my brothers, in what I recommend.
Bear with me as I explain, from beginning to end,
Why our forefathers' spirits portend,
And I also tend
To believe that the soul best suited to mend
This rift between us and our Potter's waxen "friends"
Is a living human being who often

transcends
His human condition in that, to us, he often sends
Through dispersion into the cosmic winds
His innermost thoughts to which he appends
Clear evidence that his inner self ascends
To such a level that this person is clearly a blend
Of spirit and mortal man who can obviously fend
For himself. His selection, we can easily defend:
He is a man of the spirit; he is a man of the land.
He is one with our earth and one with our sand;
He possesses great wisdom and understands
That lasting peace and tranquility undeniably demand
Impartiality, fairness, and total command

Of this complex situation that I
  propose to place in his hands.
His meditative moods and moments
  will allow him to withstand
The pressures brought to bear by us or
  Potter's renegade band.
Your hearts and souls have been
  touched by this man…
Worley Faver, it is. What do you say,
  my clan?"

The eldest of the elders stood amongst
  his peers.

"I know without hearing that our
  decision is clear.
As always, you choose wisely, it
  appears.
I speak for us all;
Go forward with your call.
Summon this spirit man; charge him
  with this task.
For a better mediator, we could not
  ask."

"Thank you all. I shall now seek the

support
Of the soldiers' ghosts and of the Potter's cohort.
Without their blessing, we must abort,
But I expect agreement without retort.
I believe they, too, realize that this is our last resort."

The chief approached the soldiers before going to the museum.
Logically, the chief knew the soldier leader would immediately see him.
Approval for Worley's selection came quickly, as one would anticipate.
When the chief asked if the soldiers wished to participate
In the mediation that was, hopefully, destined to follow,
The soldier leader's eyes welled with tears, and he tried hard to swallow.
Finally, gaining composure, he responded to the Timucuan chief.

"You and your tribe possess kindness and consideration beyond belief.
Centuries ago, you allowed us relief

By granting us asylum in Old Town.
After hearing our story, you agreed to share your sacred burial mound.
Your generosity was genuine; its impact, profound.
We trust you implicitly,
And I have the authority to state explicitly
That you shall carry our full proxy to the mediation.
We need not participate directly; I have no hesitation.
Let's pray that Potter's People possess integrity *after* the negotiation."

"My soldier spirit friend, I share your concern.
But, if there exists one living human being who can possibly discern
False or insincere testimony and attestation
From Potter's People's presentation,
It will be this human man, Worley Faver.
He will be diligent and strong; he will

not waver.
His wisdom will weave a tapestry we shall all savor.
We can have complete trust in this spirit-man Faver."

Having completed the first of his initial two tasks,
The chief telepathicized to Potter's leaders a question that asked:

"We need a brief meeting to discuss the mediator selected.
Has the spokesperson for Potter's People been elected?
If so," the message interjected,
"Shall we meet at Potter's or at my grave where I was resurrected?"

Within nanoseconds the chief almost instantly detected
The answer to the question he had projected.

"I am David Crockett. I have now been confirmed as selected

To lead our side. If you will come to
  Potter's, you will be protected.
Furthermore, we wish for previous
  impressions to be corrected
And no more transgressions on the
  land where you were resurrected.
Never again will your trust in us be
  transected."

The chief thought back
With a wisdom that most lack:

"Thank you for the consideration
Of your Potter's People's nation.
I gladly accept your invitation
As the first step in the creation
Of a constantly improving relation
Among all spirits involved in this
  equation.
When do you wish to begin your
  dissertation?"

The answer streamed back without
  deviation,

"We are prepared to move forward

The Timucuan chief grew angry and tense:

"Given that *you* are the oppressors, I take great offense
In your demanding that I present a defense
For *my* side's selection and our need to convince
Each of you. Must I remind you of all the events
Of the past few years—
The violence, the pain, the discomfort, the tears?
As a show of good faith, *your* side suggested
And your chosen leader requested
That *we* select the mediator.
There were *no* stipulations: man, spirit, ghost, or alligator.
Has your leader been replaced by an instigator?
A rebel, renegade, militant, or agitator?
A troublemaker, insurrectionist, or aggravator?

What happened to your noble negotiator
And his declarations of repentance and regret?
I must remind you, lest you forget,
That *you* and *your* figurines are in *our* debt!
My blood pressure boils!
My psyche recoils
From the thought of your presence on our soils!
You have betrayed my people and me!
Now, I cannot possibly see
How we can ever trust or believe what you say.
You have now spent your very last, final day
As poachers, squatters, and burial mound raiders.
From now on, you shall be treated as what you are: foreign invaders!
You are no longer welcome here!
Beware, you have much to fear!
One by one, we shall extract what you hold dear!

Our attacks shall renew from the flank, front, and rear.
Our strikes will not abate
Until we drive you from this city's gates!
You have until tomorrow evening at half past eight.
At that time, the sun shall set,
And you can take this bet:
If after this time, on our land you're found,
Your figurines will be melted onto our ground
And the resulting slurry dumped into St. Augustine Sound!
You have been warned! Time to be elsewhere bound!"

The chief vanished without waiting for reply.
Potter's leader Crockett could only sigh.
Potter's People's ghosts
Returned to their waxen hosts
And, despite the bravados, bold boasts,
And attempts at levity and light-hearted

joasts,
All knew it was time to vacate Florida's First Coast.

George Washington Carver - Inventor, Scientist, Educator

Chapter 16

The Ancient Elder Speaks

Crushed and disenchanted, the chief returned to his own,
All of whom already knew of the seeds he'd sown.
The Elder Council greeted their leader with an understanding tone:
They did not blame him for this failure to secure their home.
The behavior of Potter's People, none could condone.
The chief faced his group and addressed them with words sharply honed.

"I failed each of you, your spirits, and myself, too!
I lost my temper and my cool, as it was all I could do
To stand there and listen to that spiritless, ghostly crew
And realize how little they truly comprehend
Of what they already have done or where this confrontation will end!
It is a truly disappointing moment for us and our soldier friends.
I am saddened, disheartened, and now

we must contend.
I should have exercised more patience—like a white-man's saint.
I could have convinced them—if I'd only shown more restraint.
Our peace plan has been derailed
Because my temper curtailed
My self-control; my anger prevailed!
My friends, I fear I have failed!"

The most elder spirit of the council, an ancient explorer and pioneering guide,
A being who had crossed the continental bridges before the great divide,
Rose to speak. He was a confidant on whom the chief often relied.

"Cease and desist! You have absolutely not one reason to chide
Yourself for what is clearly a failure on *their* side!
Your reaction was to be expected; I must confide
That I, too, would have found it impossible to hide
My disgust and disdain for this waxing

tide
That clearly demonstrates how very wide
Is the difference between us and those beings with such false pride
That they could convince themselves that, just because they lived and died
Under unfortunate and bizarre circumstances that they deserved to reside
On our hallowed, sacred burial mounds.
Such reasoning and logic is totally unsound.
But, I have a suggestion that is more logical than profound:
You selected Worley Faver to mediate the peace.
Go! Seek him out! Have his spirit release
His feelings and beliefs about what should be done next.
Use him to quench the thoughts of failure with which you're vexed."

Chapter 17

The Chief and Worley Connect

The chief knew that, when spirit-men dream,
The soul departs the body, or so it seems.
This out-of-body experience frees the spirit-man to speak
To other souls and ghosts that hunt for, search for, or otherwise seek
Status reports about the living.
These spirit-men are intent in giving
Information to the deceased
About loved ones not yet released
From the shackles of the human form.
In fact, such communication is the norm
And helps to constantly reform
The cosmic balance between yin and yang,
Between negative and positive, and among the remnants of the Big Bang.
Interestingly, spirit-men never recall
These conversations and discussions.
They remember nothing at all,
Except, occasionally, that wonderful, weightless, floating flight

That allows them to escape gravity and fly through the night.
The spirit-men awake refreshed, rejuvenated, renewed,
And enriched by an experience enjoyed by but a very few.
Their spirituality, enriched by this interaction,
Causes their souls to glow with an internal satisfaction
That moves them ever closer to being part of a special human faction—
Humans so in tuned with the earth, the cosmos, and the eternal forces
That they gravitate to meditation and teaching philosophical courses—
Their way of bringing peace and harmony to the world and to those who will listen,
Regardless of religion, sect, or belief— with faith, they've been christened.
As you now know, even the spirits of the other life
Seek them out for advice when confronting strife.

That night, in Worley's dreams, the chief appeared
When the time of the release of Worley's spirit neared.
As his apparition ascended from Worley's human form,
A monstrous, North Florida, lightning-laden thunderstorm
Electrified the heavens and instantly transformed
This rendezvous of kindred spirits into a celestial show,
Dominated by a classic southern lights' glow
Of creeping, streaking, electrical megavolts
That deliver energy along with their thunderous jolts
To ghosts, apparitions, and even spirit-men
As they exit reality and begin to ascend.

Worley's spirit immediately sensed it was not alone.

"My Timucuan chief, I know why you

come to my home.
I am deeply honored, as I have great admiration
For the history and tradition of the Timucuan Nation,
Its people, and its underlying relation
With the Northeast Florida land that I, too, love,
Given to us through the grace and glory of the Power above."

"Yes, my son, I know you can tell.
That is good; it means 'all is well.'
You know without being told.
You possess the wisdom of age without being old.
You are calm and collected without being cold.
You are Native American kin without being 'Noled.
You shape thoughts into action without need for a mold.
You own wealth beyond belief without owning gold.
Your understanding of life exceeds

most by many million fold.
The purity of your persona is one to behold.
There is no price for which your soul could be sold.
While your meeting with me must remain untold,
I need your guidance to help me control and unfold
A plan of action that can be unrolled
And then ultimately sold
To Potter's People *and* my soul."

Worley spoke:

"For decades and centuries they've raped and ravaged
Your land and your women; they've caused catastrophic damage.
They are the ones with the heavy baggage.
Yet, they all call *you* the native 'savage.'
Now, another invader seeks safe passage.
While we all communicate with a common language,

I live by a short, simple adage:
'Do unto others as you would have them do unto you.'
Thus, I fully recognize your distrust of Potter's crew.
I only know of one modality
That can begin to address the reality
Of Potter's People's lack of morality,
Their aggressive ways, their brutality,
And their rejection of every thought of neutrality.
We must go through the formality
Of identifying any commonality
Between both groups who desire to claim this locality.
We must understand, at every level, their mentality
So that we can mitigate and eliminate their irrationality,
All the while moving toward some universality
That will bring closure and finality.
Let's view the two factions as different nationalities.
Let's focus on the major similarities

and generalities.
Let's ignore the small things and trivialities.
But let's not hesitate to challenge and debate the unrealities.
As a spirit of the living, I can avoid all partialities
In mediating this debate and ending this state of duality."

"Your approach is wise; your counsel, sage.
A similar tact we took in a prior age
When we settled our spiff with the Spanish soldiers' souls.
Our peace has lasted for centuries because we achieved our goals
Of reconciling our differences by recognizing our similarity.
Your plan brings me confidence because of my familiarity
With the results such a process can produce
When it is implemented and put to use.

I thank you my Faver spirit-man.
It is time to introduce you to Potter's clan—
Time for you to present your cogent plan."

*Davey Crockett -
Frontiersman and U.S. Congressman*

Chapter 18

Faver and Crockett Meet

The Worley man-spirit and the Timucuan chief
Shared the common thought and belief
That the elected leader of Potter's band
Was clearly the most likely to understand
The strengths and wisdoms of Worley's plan.
Using an ancient Timucuan spell,
The chief interlaced the three spirits' psyches so each could tell
What the others were thinking and, equally as well,
That there were no secrets or hidden agendas to sell.

David Crockett was stunned by the wisdom of the spirit-man,
His spirituality, and his love of the Northeast Florida land.
He immediately realized
That, in his or anyone else's eyes,
This Worley man-spirit-being
Clearly possessed the capability of seeing

A way to end the disagreeing
And of ultimately freeing
The ghosts of both sides from this debate
And this situation that would otherwise deteriorate.

The chief began:

"This Worley Faver spirit-man must mediate
A truce between our warring warrior parties
And what's left of our opposing armies."

Then, Mr. Crockett:

"Thank you for trying one last time.
My side is more than just partly wrong for these crimes.
I promise to lead,
And I will openly plead
That our side must take heed,
That our radicals cannot impede,
And that we must concede

That peaceful coexistence trumps an endless guerilla war
With its psychological and physical trauma that eats at one's core.

I repeat: our side has great need;
We *shall* take heed!
Do you wish to proceed?"

Worley's spirit took command
And revealed to them his potent plan.

"The chief's deadline is real.
His warning, he will not repeal.
Before the morning's dawn,
The battle lines will be drawn.
We three must go… *now*.
And, someway, somehow,
Within the confines of Potter's house of wax,
Lay out the suppositions and facts
That demonstrate conclusively that Potter's People lack
Any hope of prevailing in an all-out attack
Or in a prolonged terrorist war—

They already know what would be in store.

Gather your people in the auditorium.
It shall become our Exploratorium
Where your people can openly pry and probe
Every nook and cranny of my mind's globes.
The chief shall meld our minds,
All together, at one instantaneous time.
By so doing, he shall facilitate
An awareness that I will not procrastinate
As I begin to mediate
A fair and satisfactory solution for both sides.
Through the mind-lock, all shall discover that I have nothing to hide.
If you and your spirits then so decide,
The chief and I shall join in public exchange
Designed to change and rearrange
The way we think of one another
In a sincere effort to uncover

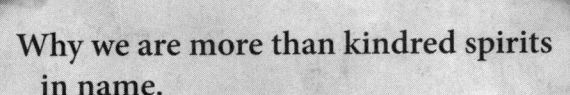

Why we are more than kindred spirits in name.
We are, in fact, very nearly the same:
More similar than not, in a sum-total game.
They shall know the Truth and the Fact:
Then it will be up to them—
compromise, retreat, or face attack.

Assemble your people! I shall be there when you call.
I shall come forthwith: I shall not stall."

Mr. Crockett made his rounds.
While a few expressed belligerence, he surprisingly found
That the majority thought the plan was creative and sound.
He began to realize that most had no desire to leave town,
Have their figurines dashed onto the ground,
Or their melted remains poured into the Sound.

Boldly renewing his control of the negotiations
And much to the dismay and consternation
Of the remaining rebels and to the elation
Of the majority of this waxen spiritual nation,
He summoned the Worley Faver spirit-man.

Moses - Religious Leader

Chapter 19

Worley Meets Potter's People

The theatre at the Potter's Wax Museum
  was packed to the gills
With the ghosts of Potter's People who
  anticipated a thrill
From seeing and meeting, for their very
  first time, a real, living spirit-man,
Especially one that brought the promise
  of a plan
To resolve the heated conflict over the
  Timucuan's sacred soils and sands
And allow them to remain on someone
  else's hallowed land.

The Timucuan chief and Worley
  materialized on Potter's stage.
In the very instant of their arrival, the
  chief immediately engaged
Each and every spirit's brain
In a mental mind-lock so no doubt
  could remain
That Worley and he were completely
  unrestrained
In the openness of their dialogue
And the facts they would catalogue
Within Worley's monologue

To demonstrate without a doubt
What mediation was all about:
Exploring common ground
With logic so sound
That a lasting solution could be found
For all these spirits of this Old Town—
One that would never come unwound.
No one needed an introduction;
No one needed instruction.
Either would have been a superfluous production.

Instead, Worley commenced:

"You know your options—it is your choice.
Mr. Crockett, Potter's People have chosen to speak with your voice.
Am I correct
In what my mind-waves detect?"

"You are, Mr. Worley Faver, spirit-man."

"Thank you. The chief possesses the proxy of his tribe and the Spanish

soldier clan.
Now, bear with me, as I reveal my plan."

"Potter's People, your leader you have chosen well.
His integrity compels me to foretell
That we need no witch's spell
To resolve this dispute
As it is easy to compute
That there is more to gain
By both factions showing refrain.

Potter's People, your choices are binary.
As defined in the dictionary,
That means there are only two
Choices for you:
Negotiate and compromise
And ultimately realize
A permanent sanctuary;
Or, be obstinate and contrary
And pen your final obituary
As the Timucuan spirits rip you asunder
Amidst a hailstorm of lightning and

thunder
Destroying your false, waxen shrines
And driving you permanently, one last time,
Into the ocean beyond our coast,
Where you will become truly lost spirits—meandering, wandering,
Purgatoried ghosts."

Worley paused as Potter's People peppered his presentation
With quizzical exclamations that expressed their consternation
About a mere mortal spirit-man's confrontation
And resulting dissertation
Concerning their current situation
Involving the native Timucuan nation.
Undaunted, Worley dispensed his hesitation
And proceeded without further procrastination.

In that instance, Potter's People suddenly knew

That this spirit-man was special—one of the chosen few—
Whose spirituality and wisdom drove them to do
Only what was fair, righteous, and true.
He spoke from his heart and from his soul.
They followed his every thought; he had control.
The following is the essence of the message his stream of consciousness told:

"Peace and tranquility are precious— far more valuable than gold.
Invading armies rarely win:
Even when they do, they pay *eternally* for their sin.
It is better to *share* something cherished,
Than to own it *alone* when you perish.
Fairness to all should be sought,
Even when *you* are the victim on whom the wrong was wrought.

You, Timucuan ghosts and Potter's

spirits, are brothers-in-arms.
You have done much damage and caused much harm.
It is time to determine if your commonalities
Can allow you to establish a single nationality
Of Timucuan spirits, Spanish military ghosts,
And Potter's People with their wax-figurine pseudo-hosts.
You share a major similarity,
Which should foster a familiarity
That disclaims either's singularity
In ownership of this peculiarity.
All parties possess a consistent background:
Common folks who are, in their simplicity, profound.
People who struggled to eke-out an existence,
Surviving any way they could on meager subsistence.
Proud people who fight for what little they have.

Considerate people who must now
  apply wisdom's salve
To mute their vociferences
And resolve their differences
In order for their culture to persist
And for them to mutually co-exist."

When Worley concluded his oration,
All in attendance from Potter's ghostly
  nation
Bowed in respect—a spiritual ovation—
For this Worley Faver spirit-man
And the wisdom of his words and his
  plan.

Compromise and tolerance comprised
  the deal—
The proclamation on the parchment was
  signed by Crockett and the chief and
  then sealed
With a shaving of wax from Crockett's
  right wrist
And a scraping of petrified blood from
  the chief's left fist
That were mixed, melted, and dripped

on the paper,
Which then disintegrated into a fog of mysterious vapor.

"You have no need for a document to memorialize your deal.
You have made the right decision; you know by how you *feel*."

The spirits sighed and then began to savor
The breath of freedom and the fruits of the labor
Of this special spirit-man, Worley Faver.
The agreement was done
With no need for guns.
Peace and calm returned
To a place where tempers once flared and burned.
The ancient spirits of Aviles Street and the ghosts of Potter's clan
Could now resume the casual hauntings that occurred before their war began—
Thanks to the work and wisdom
　　　…of the Worley Faver spirit-man.

Worley Faver - Potter
"Spirit-Man"

Chapter 20

Worley's Reward

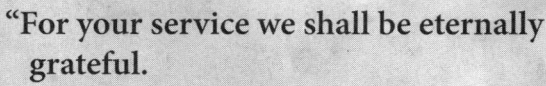

"For your service we shall be eternally grateful.
You have resolved a dispute, once violent and hateful.
You bring the promise of peace and tranquility—
An end to all our spirited hostility.
You resolved our plight when previous negotiations generated only futility.
You demonstrated the uncanny ability
To design, draw-up, and hypothesize
Scenarios that resulted in meaningful compromise.
We wish to thank you in a special way
For the exemplary service you rendered this day."

As the chief finished speaking, the Council of Elders materialized.
Worley Faver's spirit immediately realized
That he was, now, one of *them*.
In spite of different genes, he was truly next-of-kin.
The eldest elder spoke aloud, even

though all already knew
What this spirit of great wisdom was
   about to do.

"My Worley Faver spirit-man,
We wish to induct you into our clan.
Your ancestors laid the foundation for
   what you now are.
We watched them for years from near
   and far.
Their love of nature, life, and land,
   We, ourselves, observed first-hand.
Your good people protected assets we
   cherished, too.
They knew all-too-well what
   developers would do
To the pristine refuge of Pelicer Creek
   and its woods and marsh:
They would have destroyed it with a
   death sentence so harsh
That, today, nothing original or intact
   would remain.
Fortunately, your lineage possessed
   the strength to refrain
From falling victim to the lure of
   progress's wealth and powers.

They saved the sanctuary and its
  animals, its trees, its plants, and its
  flowers.
For tomorrow and all of Mankind's
  future hours
You innately understood what so few
  ever learn:
There is only one Earth; it gets no
  second turn.
Faver-Dykes Park stands as a lasting
  monument
To your people and the message their
  donation sent.

Now, it is time for you to receive your
  reward
For the peace and tranquility your
  mediation has restored
To our hallowed grounds
And our sacred burial mounds
Of St. Augustine's ancient Aviles
  Street.
As a thank for your feat,
We, the Timucuan spiritual nation,
Bequeath upon you the gift of
  Creation—

The highest level of honor we can bestow, in our estimation.
While you still labor with your human condition,
We give you our most cherished tradition:
The ability to take elements of the land—
Woods, flames, clays, and sands—
And craft great vessels, forms, and pots
That will reflect your loves, feelings, and, believe it or not,
The designs and experiences of ancient people from around the globe.
For we all share within our frontal lobes
The knowledge that we all descended from a single source—
Such knowledge has bound us together throughout history's course.
With this gift you will be compelled to create.
You will not know why, but you will *feel* this Fate.

Your pots will be prized,
But very few will realize
That your art will memorialize
The very existence of native people everywhere on earth
Who love life and land for all they're worth.
Not only that, but the perceptive few
Will touch your pots and sense history's clues
That tell of the destruction invading armies can do.
You shall be drawn inextricably back to our midst
Where you will find a way to live and exist.
As you create your art,
You shall become a greater part
Of our community,
And you shall have complete immunity
From the maladies that afflict mere mortal man:
You shall be content and complete; on your own, you shall stand.

Be blessed our Worley Faver spirit-man!
We welcome you to our Timucuan spirit-clan!"

With that proclamation, the spirits of the Timucuan nation
Vanished, and Worley awoke with much consternation,
Understanding not what had just taken place,
Recognizing not the future he faced,
And knowing only that his heart still raced.
One thought after another came at a blinding pace,
But nothing he did, either that night or after, could erase
What his heart, brain, and soul now acknowledged as true:
Worley Faver had changed and now was driven to do
What spirit-men from the beginning of time have always done:

Create great gifts of art, music, and dance for everyone;

> Great gifts to the world that cannot be undone.

Julius Caesar - Roman Emperor

WORLEY FAVER POTTERY STUDIO & GALLERY 172

Epilogue

And so it was…and it *all* came to pass,
Just as prophesized by the Timucuan spirits of the past.
Worley constructed his first pots in the late 1980s,
Using only the ancient tools available to the original American Natives.
Made of Georgia clay, his pots are built, never thrown.
His classic shapes and styles, peoples of all centuries have loved and owned.
Worley creates texture by impressing the wet clay with black walnuts or coral, alone.
He incises and carves them, then burnishes them with his special stone.
He fires them at high temperatures until they achieve the hardness of bone.
He rolls the hot vessels in sawdust to give them smoky tones.

His pots have become cherished as objects of art.
They are the essence of perfection, as they come from Worley's soul and his

heart.
And, yes, Faver's Gallery now resides at
   11A Aviles Street,
Where Worley crafts, works, and greets
Those living beings
Who sense what they are seeing:
Creations from a special man,
Blessed beyond what he or we can
   understand,
Blessed at the hands of the Timucuan
   spirit-band,
Blessed in a way so he commands
The trust and respect from all beings
   who know the mortal man.

Potter's People, the Spanish spirits, and
   Timucuan ghosts
To this day still give thanks for what
   they now cherish most:
The peace and tranquility Worley
   brought to St. Augustine's coast
By resolving the conflict among Potter's
   People and the Aviles Street ghosts—
A lasting peace that promises to
   endure—

No small accomplishment, to be sure.

As with all treaties, a few renegades refuse to concur;
So, hauntings and haintings, not infrequently, do occur:

Broken figurines and messed up hair at Potter's Wax Museum;
Visual tracers streak across video screens where anyone can see 'em;
Clairvoyants and children report the presence of a little ghost girl—
A little ghost girl lost and stranded in our strange ole world;
These and other EVPs that happen, especially at night,
And prove once and for all that Mr. Potter was right.

At the Old Military Hospital, multitudes of mournful moans
Echo through the rooms as all sorts of sordid groans—
Residual tones from ghostly patients

who were long ago cut, sawed, or sewn.
And what about those wandering instruments used by old sawbones?

At Larry's and Denise's antique shop, the site of an old jail,
The spirits often gather and one can hear them wail—
Paranormal experts proved that this is no old-wives' tale.

Even Worley's own gallery experiences disquieting events,
Which have increased in intensity with the recent advent
Of the opening of Swamp Hattie's Lair and what she represents.

As for the bright cafés and beautiful boutiques,
The stellar art galleries and the other neat shops tourists seek,
None can escape the inevitable fact:
The spirits are still here, and they're not

going back!
Remember: Aviles Street may be America's oldest road,
But long before white man came, this was the Timucuan's abode.

* * * * * * * * * * * * * * * * * * * *

Potter's People and the ancient spirits of Aviles Street,
Patrol their land to avoid repeat
Of an invasion by mortal man or marauding apparition.

Other spirits are not welcome under any condition;
Even ghosts from elsewhere in this City of Old are from the other side:
They are foreigners who wander, spook, rest, and reside
Outside the boundaries of the Timucuan's hallowed grounds.
If they trespass onto this side of Old Town,
The clacking of the "ghost meters"

announce their arrival,
But their stays are brief—it's a matter of survival.
These visitors never return because of this fear.
Trespassers, quite simply, are not welcome here.

We ourselves are the latest invading horde;
We each come here of our own accord.
They tolerate us; give thanks to the Lord,
Because we are no threat, even with our guns, knives, and swords.
We are helpless here, regardless of what we can afford.
You all now know why these spirits claim these grounds for their own.
You have read their story; you have been shown.
Please recognize their persistence that you accept their existence
As the compromise to ensure our continued peaceful coexistence

With them. It would be futile for us to put up resistance.
If these terms are not agreeable to you, you must acknowledge my insistence
That you promise to stay away and keep your distance.
Otherwise, you will betray Aviles Street's secret, silent code
And put these spirits in an agitated, aggressive, annihilative mode
By, once again, disturbing these beings of our country's oldest, most haunted road.

These beings, while living, were considered unimportant; they were the "least."
We now owe it to them to allow their souls finally to rest in peace.

The End

About the Author

"Hattie's Daddy" has been a self-proclaimed "closet poet" since his 7th grade English teacher encouraged his secret interest. His first fictional effort was *The Trilogy of Swamp Hattie*, an epic ghost tale of betrayal, revenge, Good vs Evil, love, and redemption. This work coined the nickname "Hattie's Daddy"! More recently, Dennis worked with world-renown artist Dean Mitchell to publish a truly beautiful book, *Of Southern Passions, Paintings, and Poems*, that pairs Mitchell's paintings with Dennis's poetry. Dennis is also an avid fisherman and has sold several articles about the hobby to a major outdoor magazine.

A true believer in the power of education, Hattie's Daddy serves as an emeritus member of the Committee of Visitors for Vanderbilt University's School of Engineering, the Board of Directors of Jacksonville Country Day School, and the faculty of the Young Writers' Workshop in Jacksonville. Dennis is currently the president and CEO of a Pittsburgh-based molecular cancer diagnostic company.

The Author
"Hattie's Daddy"
Dennis M. Smith, Jr., M.D.

Other Books
by Dennis M. Smith Jr., M.D.

Now Available

The Trilogy of Swamp Hattie:
A hideous St. Augustine ghost's epic tale of betrayal, revenge, and Good versus Evil illustrated with more than 75 original works of art created specifically for the book!

Of Southern Passions, Paintings, and Poems: Internationally acclaimed artist Dean Mitchell, described by one art critic as a "modern-day Vermeer," and poet Dennis Smith collaborated to produce this magnificent 300-page book that features Dean's paintings and Dennis's poetry. This incredible collection of artwork, which includes watercolors, acrylics, and oils and covers subject matter ranging from southern scenes to urban sites to magnificent portraits of black people, inspired Dennis's verses. This magical combination creates a uniquely beautiful book that provides not just the striking images of the artist and poignant writing of the poet but also personal insights into their minds, inner souls, and creativity. Fittingly, Dr. Robert Steele, Executive Director of the Driskell Center at the University of Maryland, describes this book as "…a work of art itself."

Coming Next
"These books are on the editor's desk now!"

The Mystery of the Mill Creek Mud Monster: A good guardian monster, an evil phantom wolf, a lost little girl—chance casts them together—can fate, faith, and the Mud Monster save her?

The Witches of Cattle Creek Crossing: Ravaged by swamp-water fever, old St. Augustine's children mysteriously disappear, and the town's citizens seek revenge and retribution on six swamp witch sisters!

Gallery of Potter's People

Here are the images of a few of the figurines that can be seen at Potter's Wax Museum, the first museum of its kind established in the United States. This exhibit, its incredible figurines, and its reputation for its haunts, haints, and ghosts inspired this novel.

Abraham Lincoln
16th President of the United States

Benjamin Franklin
Author, Printer, Political Theorist

Henry VIII
King of England

Joan of Arc
Heroine of France

Hirohito
Emperor of Japan

Winston Churchill
*Prime Minister
of the United Kingdom*

Ulysses S. Grant
*Union General
18th President of the United States*

Napoleon
Emperor of France

Mussolini
Italian Dictator

Michelangelo
Sculptor, Painter, Architect

Edgar Allan Poe
Author and Poet

Saint Joseph
Earthly Father of Jesus Christ

Robert E. Lee
Confederate General

Al Capone
American Gangster

Hitler
Nazi Dictator and Murderer

Teddy Roosevelt
26th President of the United States

Samuel Clemens
Author
"Mark Twain"

Joseph Stalin
Dictator of Soviet Union

Mary I
Queen of England
"Bloody Mary"

Leonardo Da Vinci
Artist, Inventor, Scientist

George Washington Carver
Inventor, Scientist, Educator

Davey Crockett
*Frontiersman
and U.S. Congressman*

Moses
Religious Leader

Worley Faver
Artist & Potter
"Spirit-Man"

Julius Caesar
Roman Emperor

Aviles Street Merchants Association

Antiques & Uniques Collectibles
7 Aviles Street

Ancient Aviles Ghost Trek
7 Aviles Street

Bouvier Maps & Prints
11E Aviles Street

Natural Reflections Glass Gallery
11F Aviles Street

Hookey Hamilton Photography
25 Aviles Street

Joel Bagnal Goldsmith
11B Aviles Street

Restaurant and Cafe Sol Brasileirissimo
8 Aviles Street

Worley Faver Pottery Studio & Gallery
11A Aviles Street

Swamp Hattie's Lair
11A Aviles Street
(Inside Worley Faver Pottery)

Potter's Wax Museum
17 King Street

Ghost Tours of St Augustine, Inc.
123 Saint George Street

iMakeThat
www.imakethat.com

Local Legends Press
www.locallegendspress.com

Local Legends Press
www.LocalLegendsPress.com

digital artists
iMakeThat
www.imakethat.com

Old Town St. Augustine

Old North City Gate

Castillo de San Marco "Old Fort"

Matanzas Bay

Sebastian River

N

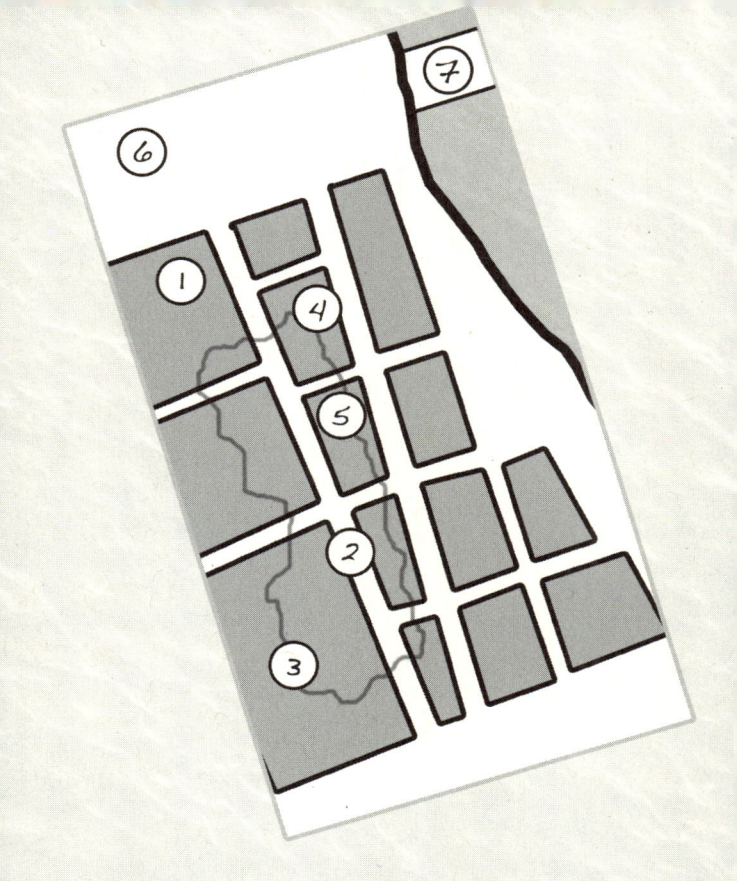

1 Potter's Wax Museum
2 Aviles Street
3 Timucuan Burial Mounds
4 Old Spanish Military Hospital
5 Worley Faver Pottery Studio & Gallery
6 Plaza
7 Bridge of Lions
8 King Street
9 San Marco Avenue
10 Charlotte Street
11 St. George Street
12 Spanish Street

Potter's People